Luke's jaw dropped down to his knees when he realized a gangling, galloping goalkeeper was charging upfield to join in the fun. The Zebras could not believe their eyes either. The bright, multi-coloured top stood out clearly from the other shirts and their defensive organization fell apart. Nobody knew who was to mark him.

'Get back, Sanjay, get back!' Luke screamed, glancing fearfully at the Swifts' empty goal. 'What are you doing here? Have you gone mad?'

It was too late. Brain whipped the corner over, curling the ball in towards the near post. Sanjay timed his arrival perfectly and barely had to jump. He brushed past an uncertain challenger and sent a bullet header screaming over the full-back who was guarding the line . . .

THE BIG PRIZE
Rob Childs

*'Huh! Some lucky mascot you're gonna be –
Selworth have got no chance this afternoon with
you around!'*

Everything seems to be going great for Chris
Weston. First he wins the prize of being chosen
to be the mascot for the local football league club
for their next F.A. Cup match. Then he is picked
to play in goal for his school team on the morning of the same day.

But then disaster strikes and Chris can hardly
walk, let alone run out on to a pitch. Has his luck
suddenly changed for the worse? And will he
miss his chance of being a mascot?

A lively and action-packed new title in a popular
series about two football-mad brothers.

0 552 528234

HERE WE GO!
Diane Redmond

We stared at him, incredulous. He MUST have got it wrong. We COULDN'T be playing LAST SEASON'S LEAGUE CHAMPIONS . . .

With a headmaster like 'Floppy' Fairweather, a great believer in anti-competitive sports, no-one at Moorside school has ever played much football. They don't even know the rules! But Danny, Tamz, Imran and the other kids who volunteer to make up the school's first ever football team quickly discover just how much fun the game can be. Not only that but they can't wait to get out there, start playing and WIN. Even if their first opponents are last season's league champions . . .

A terrific and fast-paced footballing tale, packed with fun and action, from the very first kick-off to the final whistle of the last vital Cup match of the season.

0 440 863260

ALL GOALIES ARE CRAZY. . .

. . .BUT SOME GOALIES ARE
MORE CRAZY THAN OTHERS!

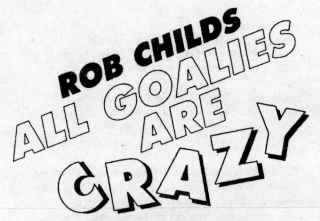

ROB CHILDS
ALL GOALIES ARE CRAZY

... BUT SOME GOALIES ARE MORE CRAZY THAN OTHERS!

ILLUSTRATED BY
AIDAN POTTS

CORGI YEARLING BOOKS

ALL GOALIES ARE CRAZY
A CORGI YEARLING BOOK : 0 440 86350 3

First publication in Great Britain

PRINTING HISTORY
Corgi Yearling edition published 1996
Reprinted 1997

Copyright © 1996 by Rob Childs
Illustrations copyright © 1996 by Aidan Potts
Cover illustration by Derek Brazell

Set in 12/15pt Linotype Century Schoolbook by
Phoenix Typesetting, Ilkley, West Yorkshire

Corgi Yearling Books are published by Transworld Publishers Ltd,
61–63 Uxbridge Road, London W5 5SA,
in Australia by Transworld Publishers (Australia) Pty Ltd,
15–25 Helles Avenue, Moorebank, NSW 2170
and in New Zealand by Transworld Publishers (NZ) Ltd,
3 William Pickering Drive, Albany, Auckland.

The Random House Group Limited supports The Forest Stewardship
Council® (FSC®), the leading international forest-certification organisation.
Our books carrying the FSC label are printed on FSC®-certified paper.
FSC is the only forest-certification scheme supported by the leading
environmental organisations, including Greenpeace. Our
paper procurement policy can be found at
www.randomhouse.co.uk/environment

MIX
Paper from
responsible sources
FSC® C018072

Printed and bound in Great Britain by Clays Ltd, St Ives plc

Especially for all crazy goalies – like me!

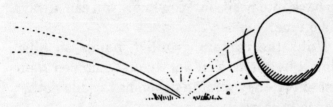

1 The One and Only

It looked a certain goal. The ball swerved and dipped as it flew towards the target, an inviting expanse of unguarded netting.

Matthew, the school team captain, let out a groan of dismay, angry at himself for failing to block the shot. Nothing could stop it going in now. Suddenly, a blur of bright colours flashed across his line of sight, deflecting the speeding missile at the last possible moment up and over the crossbar to safety.

'Sanjay!' Matthew cried out. 'Where did you come from?'

The gangly goalkeeper sprawled on the ground, his grin almost as wide as the goal itself. Sanjay lay like that for several seconds, as if posing for a posse of photographers, before springing up onto his feet. 'No sweat!' he smirked, tugging his crumpled, multi-coloured top back into position. 'You know you can always rely on me.'

'Huh!' the captain grunted, hands on hips. 'That'll be the day. If you hadn't fumbled their first effort, they wouldn't even have had another chance to score.'

'Saved it, didn't I?'

Matthew could hardly argue with that. The applause from the smattering of spectators was still continuing and Sanjay soaked it all up.

'Dead brill save, Sanjay!' yelped an excited voice. It came from behind a bobbing camcorder rapidly heading towards them around the pitch.

None of the home players needed to guess who was trying to film and talk at the same time. Everyone in Year 8 of Swillsby Comprehensive knew the sound and sight of soccer-mad Luke Crawford. In fact, most of the pupils in other year groups had heard of him too.

'Keep out of the way, Loony Luke,' Matthew warned him. 'We don't want you here putting us off with that thing.'

Luke's thin, flushed face appeared round the camera, looking hurt. 'Only trying to help, recording the game so you can see what went wrong.'

Matthew scowled. 'Nothing's gone wrong, thanks very much. At least not until you turned up. It's still nil–nil.'

'Won't be for long, if you don't watch out,' Luke replied cheekily. 'They're taking the corner.'

The captain whirled round. 'C'mon, men, mark up!' he shouted.

Too late. The ball was whipped low across the penalty area straight to an unmarked attacker lurking just outside the six-yard box. He hit it first time before any of the defenders could react, but Sanjay's reflexes were sharper. He flung himself instinctively towards the danger and the ball smacked him full in the face, his hands unable to parry it.

The goalkeeper had done his duty. He had successfully protected his goal once more, but it was a little while before the game could go on. Sanjay needed some running repairs.

'Frosty' Winter, Swillsby's long-suffering sports teacher and short-sighted referee, cleaned up the boy's bloodied nose with a sponge of cold water. 'There, as handsome as ever!' he lied.

'What a hero!' laughed Adam, the centre-back. 'But try and catch it in your mouth next time, will you? You've given away another corner!'

Sanjay attempted a grin, but it was a bit too sore. He gingerly ran his tongue around his teeth to check they were all present and correct.

'Do you want to carry on?' asked Frosty.

13

Sanjay looked at the teacher as if it was the most stupid question he had ever heard. 'Sure. Just a bang in the face, that's all. I'm OK.'

Frosty shook his head. 'Must be true, that old saying.'

'What's that, sir?' asked Sanjay, half-guessing what was coming.

'All goalies are crazy!'

'They have to be,' Matthew sneered, 'the way they risk getting their fingers broken, head smashed in and teeth kicked out every match.'

Luke put down the camcorder to fetch the water bucket off the pitch and show his support for his pal's bravery. Sanjay also played for Swillsby Swifts, Luke's lowly Sunday League team. 'Great stuff, Sanjay. You're the best keeper we've got.'

Matthew pulled a face. 'He's the *only* one. Nobody else in the squad is crazy enough to want to play in that position.'

Sanjay knew that the captain wasn't exactly his greatest fan. 'Guess that makes me the best, then, doesn't it?' he replied wryly.

Thanks to more saves from Sanjay, missed chances and good defending by both sides, the

match remained goal-less until soon after half-time.

That was the moment when Jon Crawford, Luke's talented cousin, chose to display his silky-smooth skills. Receiving the ball wide on the left, he shaped to turn one way but floated past his bemused marker the other. Jon glanced up to see the keeper straying off his line and curled a shot with the inside of his right foot tantalisingly over the poor lad's outstretched, groping fingers. An exquisite goal.

Luke could not have done it better himself. In fact, he could not have done anything like it at all, if he had tried for a hundred years. Instead, perhaps recognizing his own limitations as a footballer, Luke did the next best thing. He acted out his fantasy of being a budding sports reporter and live commentator, feverishly describing the drama in words for his imagined nationwide audience as he filmed the action.

'Jon Crawford, Swillsby's Johan Cruyff, the flying Dutchman, sells a sensational dummy to make the defender look a fool. Jon now moves inside, creating space for a pop at goal, picks his spot and shoots. It looks good – it is good – GOOOAAALLL! Jon Crawford has done it again . . .'

16

'Who is this Joanne Cruyff you're always raving about?'

The sudden demand startled Luke enough to interrupt his commentary. He looked around in disgust at the questioner. It was Tubs, slouching, hands in pockets, on the touchline. He was another Swifts' player who, like most of them, could not claim a regular place in the school side.

'It's not Joanne, it's pronounced Yo-han,' Luke corrected him sternly, cross that his hero had been maligned through ignorance or deliberate cheek. Probably the latter, he realized, coming from Tubs.

'Yo, man!' Tubs grinned.

Luke wasn't amused. '*Yohan*, but spelt with a J,' he stressed. 'It's Dutch, see, and – since you ask – Johan Cruyff was the finest footballer ever to grace the turf of the world's biggest and best soccer stadiums!'

'OK, OK, save the poetry for your match reports,' laughed Tubs. 'You reckon Jon plays a bit like him, do you?'

Luke shrugged, just like his laid-back cousin might have done. 'Sometimes, when he's in the mood.'

'Yeah, that's his trouble. Magic one moment

and then disappears from view like the Invisible Man.'

'He can win his team the game in that one moment, though,' Luke defended him. 'Just like he has done today.'

'I shouldn't bank on it,' Tubs said, pointing down the other end. 'Look, they've broken clean through our defence straight from the kick-off. They're going to equalize.'

'Not with Sanjay playing like he is . . .' Luke began. 'Oops!'

The attacker had mis-hit his shot, sending the ball skidding along the ground. Sanjay appeared to have it covered comfortably, but somehow let the ball slip through his hands and into the net.

'I don't believe it!' cried Luke. He knew the keeper had his good and bad days, but this had seemed to be one of his better ones. Luke took his disappointment out on Tubs. 'I've missed that goal now, thanks to you keeping me here talking. We haven't got it on tape to study later.'

Tubs let loose his loud, rumbling laugh. 'I reckon Sanjay will thank me as well when he finds out. He won't have wanted to see that again.'

Sanjay was too busy trying to make his

apologies to worry about action replays. 'Sorry, you guys. The ball bobbled up just in front of me.'

'You mean you took your eye off it,' Matthew complained. 'Typical! You've just gone and wasted all our hard work to take the lead.'

'Lay off him, Matt,' Jon interrupted. 'If it wasn't for Sanjay, we'd have been getting slaughtered by now.'

'He's just cancelled out your goal. Aren't you bothered?'

Jon shrugged casually. 'Well, guess we'll just

have to go and score another one, won't we?'

Sadly, it wasn't to be quite that simple. Growing in confidence, the visitors laid siege to Sanjay's crowded penalty area and Swillsby barely even managed another decent attempt on goal, never mind score. They were struggling to hold on for a draw, hoping Frosty would blow the final whistle to rescue them.

'How much longer, sir?' panted Matthew.

'You'll find out soon enough,' Frosty replied gruffly without checking his watch. 'Just keep your mind on the game.'

Luke, too, was hard at work, beavering away along the touchline. *'Inside the final minute, the ball is once more with Sanjay Mistry, Swillsby's eccentric goalie. He's hoping to use up extra precious seconds, dribbling it out of his area, taunting the opposition to come and make him hurry. The number eleven is taking the bait – Sanjay really ought to be kicking the ball away now ... Oh, no! He's starting to show off, trying to keep possession over near the touchline, shielding the ball from the winger – he's lost it!'*

Luke dried up in horror. His head jerked up from the camera in time to see the panicking goalkeeper clatter crudely into the winger from

behind in his desperation to regain the ball, but the damage had already been done. The ball was gone and Sanjay was left stranded way out of his goal.

The centre-forward pounced on the loose ball and had the easiest of tasks to slide home the vital second goal. The scorer wheeled away into the arms of his delighted teammates while the Swillsby players stood staring at Sanjay in shock. Some threw themselves to the ground, unable to face up to what had happened.

There was not even time for the game to re-start, and the final three cheers from Matthew were decidedly half-hearted.

'Oh, well,' Sanjay sighed heavily. 'You win some, lose some.'

He was speaking to himself. At least for the moment, nobody was talking to him. But he knew for certain they would all eventually have one or two things to say – and he wasn't looking forward to that very much . . .

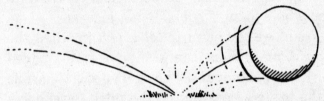

2 The Seven Commandments

Luke took his roles as captain, player-manager, chief coach and trainer of Swillsby Swifts very seriously. It was, after all, *his* team – even if the names of his dad and uncle were on the official forms.

At the Swifts' mid-week practice session, he hoped to pass on some useful tips to Sanjay. Since the disasters of the last school match, Luke had been reading up all about goalkeeping from the various coaching manuals that cluttered the shelves of soccer books in his bedroom.

First, though, before leaving the changing cabin to brave the chilly village recreation ground, he wanted words with everybody. 'We've been giving too many goals away, men. We've got to tighten up in defence.'

'Why pick on us, Skipper?' asked Big Ben, their giraffe-necked, bespectacled centre-half. 'The whole team is rubbish, not just us.'

'Yeah, we're bound to let a few in when the opposition pitches camp in our half,' added Mark, his partner at the back. 'I've even seen one goalie bring a book out on the pitch to read 'cos he had nothing else to do.'

'That's not true,' Luke insisted. 'Is it? What was he reading?'

Mark laughed. 'Dunno. Nobody got near enough to him to see.'

'Probably a book on how to overcome loneliness,' Sanjay cackled.

'Not something you'll ever suffer from, is it, playing for the school and the Swifts,' Tubs guffawed.

'I don't mind being kept busy. Gives me plenty of practice and helps me improve,' Sanjay replied and then grinned, realizing why everyone had started laughing. 'Well, anybody can make mistakes.'

'Yeah,' Mark put in, 'but it must take loads of practice to make such good ones all the time.'

Luke felt he was losing control of this team talk. 'Look, forget that now, it's ancient history. And, anyway, we're not rubbish, Big Ben. We're getting better every match.'

'True,' Tubs nodded, as if serious for a moment. 'We're only losing by single figures now, not double!'

Luke took up the point, missing the irony. 'Exactly. Now if we're more organized in defence, we can keep the goals down and maybe even score a few ourselves from counter-attacks on the break.'

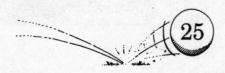

Big Ben frowned. 'Have you been reading those coaching books of yours again, Skipper?'

'Actually I've been reading *Animal Farm* by George Orwell.'

There was a groan from Dazza, the Swifts' right winger. 'We're having to study that in English this term. It's all about pigs and stuff.'

'Well, there's a bit more to it than that,' said Luke. 'It's brill. You can learn a lot from it, even though it was published back in 1945.'

'That's over fifty years ago,' gasped Big Ben. 'Now who's talking about ancient history!'

Luke ignored him. 'These animals take over a

farm, see, led by the pigs because they're the most intelligent . . .'

Tubs interrupted. 'Er, does this have anything to do with football, Skipper? Only I wouldn't mind having the chance to kick a ball about a bit before it gets too dark to see where I'm kicking it.'

'Of course it does, just listen a minute. Snowball showed that . . .'

'Snowball?' queried Mark.

Dazza answered. 'He's one of the pig leaders.'

'Glad to know you're paying some attention in class,' remarked Luke. 'Well, this Snowball was dead clever, full of ideas, and he planned their tactics for when the humans tried to get the farm back. He showed how to turn defence into attack, catch the enemy off guard and pull off a great victory. It was called the *Battle of the Cowshed*!'

The players broke into almost uncontrollable giggles at that and it was a while before they calmed down enough for Mark to speak. 'Has this by any chance, Skipper, got something to do with all these posters that have suddenly appeared in here?'

Luke nodded and smiled with satisfaction as the players' eyes travelled round the cabin walls. 'Glad you've noticed them at last. I put them up

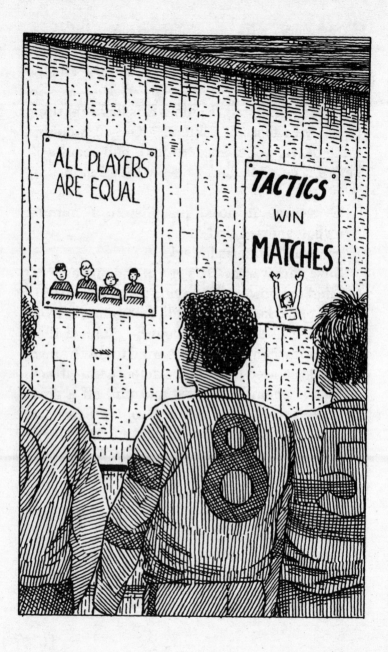

to motivate everybody to do their best.'

'*Be Determined*,' Mark read out the wording on the neatly printed poster above his head, starting the others off.

'*Work Hard, Play Hard*,' Big Ben announced from another.

'*Tactics Win Matches*,' joined in Gary, quickly followed by his identical twin.

'*Teamwork Triumphs*,' Gregg chortled.

'What's this one? *The Referee Is Always Right*!' Tubs snorted. 'Unless it's Frosty, you mean!'

Brain, the Swifts' dyslexic left winger, peered at one poster nearby and shook his head in bemusement. 'There are times like this when I'm quite glad I don't read too well.'

Sanjay did the honours for him. 'It says, *Play To The Final Whistle*. That's worth knowing, eh?'

'Huh! I think I recognize this last one, Skip,' Dazza grunted. '*All Players Are Equal*. That's from *Animal Farm*, right?'

'Dead right,' Luke beamed. 'Snowball put *animals* of course in *his* Seven Commandments, but I reckon it applies to all players in a team too.'

Sanjay grinned. 'Even when one of them is

player-manager – plus captain, coach and any other title he fancies . . . Skipper?'

'Yeah, well,' Luke mumbled. 'I mean, you've got to have some sort of leader, haven't you? The pigs soon made sure the other animals knew that.'

'Was this pig Snowball a good footballer as well?' asked Big Ben.

'Doubt it. Probably a bit too fat, I should think.'

'Like Tubs, you mean?' Sanjay put in, never slow to miss a chance to tease the roly-poly full-back. 'He eats like a pig!'

Tubs took the jibe in good spirit as usual. 'Playing for a team called *Swillsby* Swifts, I reckon it's just as well people nickname us the Sloths instead of the Pigs!'

'What happened to Snowball in the end?' asked Mark.

'That was sad,' sighed Luke. 'The rival pigs got too jealous of him and drove him away.'

'I wonder why?' Tubs remarked drily. 'Perhaps they got fed up listening to him going on and on all the time . . .'

The Swifts were rescued by Luke's Uncle Ray who threw open the cabin door. 'C'mon, get

cracking, lads. I haven't been blowing up all these footballs for nothing. Let's see some action round here.'

Luke took the hint. He quickly organized a training game for most of the squad where the attackers worked to find ways of breaking down the defence. With defenders like the Swifts had, that wasn't too difficult. The hardest part for the equally inept attackers was getting their own shots on target. There was scarcely any need for a goalkeeper and Luke left his dad to stand between the posts and supervise the session.

Luke had other plans for Sanjay. He took him down to the far end of the pitch with the Garner twins in order to give the erratic keeper some extra individual coaching. Gary and Gregg began hitting a string of centres high and low into the goalmouth for Sanjay to come off his line and try to gather them cleanly.

'C'mon, Dracula, grab hold of this one,' shouted Gary, as he swept the ball into the goalmouth at catchable height.

Sanjay made a mess of it. He timed his jump well, but totally missed the ball. It sailed between his flailing hands and would have given any attacker behind him a simple headed goal.

Luke sighed as Sanjay pretended to look for holes in his luminous green, goalie gloves. 'Not heard him called that before. Why Dracula?'

"Cos he hates crosses!' Gregg laughed. 'We just made it up!'

'Ha, ha, very funny,' Luke groaned. 'C'mon, Sanjay, never mind those two idiots. Eyes on the ball and keep those hands together. Get them right behind it.'

'Think you can do any better, Skipper?' he asked sarcastically. 'Want to demonstrate how it's done?'

'No, I'm just encouraging you, that's all.'

'Well, don't. I do things my own way, right?'

'You certainly do,' muttered Luke under his breath, but Sanjay caught it – about the only thing he had caught so far.

'What did you say?'

Luke thought quickly. 'I just said, "I'll leave it to you", OK?'

'Hmm . . .' Sanjay murmured, not amused. He loved his goalkeeping and was getting a bit narked by all the recent criticism. 'You'd better do as well. Just don't start interfering.'

Luke had brought along some mathematical charts he'd produced on his home computer to

show Sanjay how goalkeepers can successfully narrow the shooting angles in one-against-one situations. Right now, though, he doubted whether Sanjay would really appreciate such advice and he wisely decided to leave the diagrams in his bag.

Sanjay's performance did nothing to renew anybody's faith in his abilities. Luke and the twins had never seen him mishandle the ball so often, and he also played badly when they joined the others for a final seven-a-side game.

'He seems to have lost confidence completely since those mistakes cost the school that game,' Luke mused. 'This is serious . . .'

For once, Luke was quite right. Sanjay was a bag of nerves in their next Sunday game, nothing like his usual jokey, happy-go-lucky self. His frequent mistakes gave the rest of the defence the jitters, too, whenever the ball went near him and the Swifts crashed to yet another heavy defeat, 8–1. The only bright spot for the team was their goal, an equalizer by Gregg, before the defensive dam burst and the flood-gates opened once more.

Luke's gloomy mood wasn't helped by his own horrendous game at centre-forward. He was

glad Dad hadn't filmed the action. It would have been difficult to edit out all the howlers he made himself, never mind Sanjay's. Worst of all was that open goal he missed, somehow scooping the ball against a post and then heading the rebound wide.

As always, he entered the sorry details of the match into his little black notebook in red ink, recording the result, the scorer and the team. He ended his match report somewhat wistfully:

Perhaps our worst display so far. Can't even strengthen our side with new signings – nobody else wants to play for us. I wonder what Snowball would have done in this situation . . . ?

3 Who's in Goal?

'What about me having a go in goal for the school?'

His cousin's question jolted Jon out of a daydream. 'You? In goal?'

'Don't say it like that,' Luke complained. 'You make it sound as if the sun would switch its light out and go off on holiday.'

'Sorry, Luke. I'm just gobsmacked, that's all. I'd never even thought about it before.'

'Neither had I till the other day. But the way Sanjay's playing . . .'

Jon nodded. 'True. You could hardly do any worse, I guess.'

'You wanta bet!' Luke laughed. 'You've seen what I'm like here.'

They looked at Luke's home-made wooden goal and Jon smiled. 'Well, yes, you're not quite the greatest goalie in the world, I must admit.'

'I'm not even the greatest goalie in my own back garden. That old gnome stops more shots than I do when we stick him on the goal-line!'

'So why do you suddenly want to play in goal for the Comp?'

'Well, Sanjay challenged me to prove I could do better, and I'm tempted to call his bluff. Nobody else ever wants to keep goal and I think a bit of competition might do him good. Keep him on his toes.'

Jon gave his usual little shrug. 'Could work. And, anyway, even if it doesn't, you might end up getting picked for the team instead of him.'

Luke grinned. 'That had crossed my mind. But I can see three snags. The main one is that I love *scoring* goals, not stopping them – even if I'm not much cop at doing either!'

'And what's the second?'

'Frosty! He wouldn't dare risk putting me in goal. He's tearing his hair out already with Sanjay. I'd send him completely bald!'

'That should be worth watching,' Jon smirked. 'And the third?'

Luke sighed. 'Old Dracula himself! Sanjay won't like having a rival.'

'He'll have to lump it. Won't do him any harm to have to fight for his place at last. Make him buck his ideas up. He's had it too cushy.'

'Don't suppose he'll appreciate I'm really doing this for his sake – and the Swifts' of course,' Luke said. 'He won't see it like that.'

'Tough. Anyway, you could still play centre-forward on Sundays, if you wanted to,' Jon suggested. 'Best of both worlds, I reckon, as player-manager. It'd give you the choice of where you think the Swifts need you most in a game – in goal or up front.'

Luke liked the sound of that, and already his football fantasies began to unfold in his fertile imagination. There he was, pulling off brilliant saves in goal before swapping shirts to wear his favourite number nine and scoring the winning goal himself. Grabbing the glory at both ends!

He trotted over to fetch their ball from the shrubbery where his last shot had sent it, and then took up position between the goalposts. 'OK, Johan, let me have it,' he ordered rashly,

39

rolling the ball out to his cousin. 'This could be the start of a brand new soccer career . . .'

Jon was the school team's leading scorer and had a lethal, accurate shot with either foot. He struck the ball this time with his right while it was still moving and lashed it at the target.

'. . . or perhaps not . . .' Luke sighed as he lay flat out on the lawn, the leather ball quietly mocking his ambitions in the corner of the net.

'Right, who's in goal, then?' asked Frosty as the boys milled about before the start of an eight-a-side practice game.

Sanjay felt he didn't need to put his hand up. He began to wander over towards one set of posts automatically.

'Besides Sanjay, I mean,' the teacher muttered, knowing that nobody would volunteer. 'C'mon, you lot, just for one goal, and then someone else has a turn.'

The players didn't like that system. Some of them deliberately let a goal in straight away so they could go back out on the pitch, a selfish action not appreciated by the rest of their team.

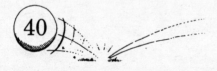

Jon glanced at Luke, who swallowed, plucked up the courage needed to risk Frosty's ridicule and slowly raised his hand.

'What's the matter now?' Frosty snapped. 'You should have remembered to go before you came out here!'

'I don't want the toilet,' said Luke as the others laughed. 'I'd like to be in goal.'

The look on Frosty's face! The colour drained from his chubby cheeks and he seemed to age five years before he realized they must be trying to pull his leg. 'OK, nice joke, lads. Luke had me going there for a minute. Which one of you put him up to that?'

Only by their own shocked reactions did Frosty sense that Luke must be serious. 'You're telling me that you want to try out in goal?'

Luke nodded and Frosty gulped. Try as he might, he hadn't found a way to deter Luke from turning up to every practice, even though he was rarely rewarded with a game in the school's black and white stripes. The squad was so small, the teacher sometimes had to pick Luke to make up the numbers, but he still regarded the boy's unco-ordinated efforts as a potential liability. His wayward, over-enthusiastic running was guaranteed to upset the balance of the team like a loose cannon on the deck of a ship rolling in a storm.

It was Jon in the end who forced his hand. 'C'mon, sir, it won't hurt. It's only a practice. Why not let him have a go?'

Frosty could see no way out of it. 'Right, he can be on your side, then. He's your responsibility.'

Jon and Matthew chose the rest of their players as Luke bounced a ball up and down nearby, avoiding Sanjay's eye. 'One good thing about this goalkeeping lark,' he murmured to himself. 'At least I haven't got left till last as usual. I was first pick!'

'C'mon, team,' Luke heard Matthew call out.

'Shoot from anywhere. As long as it's on target, it'll go in. Loony Luke can't stop a bus!'

Luke refused to be intimidated by the captain's taunts. But as the game kicked off, it felt very strange to be standing underneath the crossbar, somehow lonely and vulnerable. It looked such a different game from this viewpoint that he didn't even do his habitual commentary. He decided to do some shouting instead. He'd read somewhere about the value to a team of a goalkeeper who yelled instructions and encouragement to his fellow defenders.

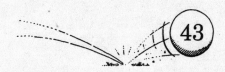

'Watch that man, Gary. Mark him!' he bawled out, making one or two players jump in surprise. 'Yours, Big Ben, go on, go in hard. Good man. Well tackled. Now clear it. Out, defence, out!'

Big Ben and the twins were the only other Swifts at the practice, but Luke's status as their Sunday skipper was not in evidence here. 'Belt up, will you, Luke!' complained Gary. 'You're giving us all earache!'

But Luke meant to make sure his shrill voice was heard by everybody, including Sanjay right at the far end. 'They're coming again, defence. Mark tight!' he demanded. 'Don't give them space. Close them down.'

Only the shot shut him up. Matthew himself let fly from the edge of the penalty area and the ball screamed Luke's way, knocking his fingers back with its power as he tried to keep it out. He failed, leaving him with a sore hand for his pains.

'*Goooaaalll!*' Matthew cackled, mercilessly imitating Luke's own commentary style. '*The keeper had it covered, but he couldn't stop it.*'

There was no net on the goal to do so either. Luke trailed away to the hedge to retrieve the ball, cursing all the mocking behind him but

determined not to show that his fingers were hurting like mad.

'One–nil!' Matthew chanted as Luke returned with the ball, putting it down for a goal-kick to re-start the game. Frosty didn't bother with centres in practices.

Luke had never previously taken a goal-kick and wasn't quite sure where to aim it. Everybody seemed to be marked until he saw Jon moving into space on the wing. Luke ran up to the ball and tried to lift it over the players grouped around the edge of the area.

The idea was right but the execution wasn't. Luke didn't possess the necessary power. He scuffed his kick and sent the ball straight to Matthew who chested it down and blasted it back at the goal. Luke could only watch helplessly as the ball sped past him, but it veered away to strike the far post and bounded towards him again like an obedient dog. He could hardly believe his luck and hugged the ball in delight before responding to Jon's cries upfield.

Luke amazed himself with the success of his drop-kick. He connected with the ball cleanly and sent it whirling away up to his cousin, catching the opponents off-guard. Jon easily eluded

the single defender and advanced on goal, forcing Sanjay to come out towards him.

It was no contest. Jon loved this kind of situation and always fancied his chances of being able to dribble the ball round a goalkeeper. He slowed, waited until Sanjay committed himself with his weight on his right leg and then whipped the ball past him on the left, throwing him completely off balance.

Jon didn't even score immediately. He stopped the ball right on the line, resting the sole of his boot on top of it, teasing the keeper. 'Want to come and dive on it, Sanjay?'

'Just knock it in and get it over with,' the keeper growled, sitting on his haunches. 'You've made your point.'

Jon rolled the ball over the line to finish the job and then placed it in the six-yard box himself for Sanjay to hoof it back into play. 'One–all, I reckon,' Jon chuckled as he passed Matthew.

'Not for long,' Matthew grinned. He and Jon were also teammates for a top Sunday side, Padley Panthers, and both boys were very glad they didn't have the same goalkeeping problem there as well. 'Let's see who's got the biggest clown in goal – Count Dracula or Loony Luke!'

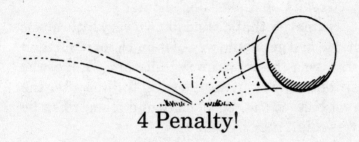

4 Penalty!

Luke's performance in goal was not quite as disastrous as Frosty and the other players had expected.

It was bad, but not so bad that he had to be replaced. He stayed in for the whole game, his side losing 5–3, but Luke found ample compensation for the five goals in the one good save he managed to pull off.

Gary had planted the ball smack on to his brother's head from the left wing and as Gregg nodded it down, it fell just right for Adam. The big centre-back had joined the attack, too, eager to grab a goal himself at Luke's expense, and he hammered the ball in full stride. Dead straight. Its force literally knocked Luke off his feet. As he tried to struggle back up, gasping for the breath that had exploded from his body, he realized he was sitting on something – the football!

'Great stop, Luke!' Jon shouted.

No matter that he had known very little about it. He had got in the way of it and kept it out, and that was the most important thing. Luke was still proudly re-living his save, trailing after the rest back to the school changing room, when he was confronted by Sanjay.

'So what's the big idea?'

'What do you mean?' asked Luke, stalling for time.

'You being goalie. You trying to cramp my style?'

'No, I just wanted to find out what it really felt like to play there.'

Sanjay eyed him suspiciously. 'Are you planning to drop me and play in goal yourself for the Swifts?'

Luke looked shocked. 'Course not. You're our keeper, Sanjay, but . . .'

'But what?'

'Well, what if you couldn't play one game, or got injured or something? I mean, we haven't got any reserve keeper, have we? Somebody would have to take your place. Somebody with at least a bit of experience . . .'

Sanjay wasn't satisfied. 'Look, if you don't think I'm any good, just say so and I'll clear off and play for some other team instead.'

'C'mon, Sanjay, don't talk like that. You're the best, you know that. There's nothing sinister going on behind your back.'

They reached the school and Sanjay leant on the wall to remove his boots while Luke plonked

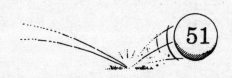

51

himself on the concrete. Jon popped his head out of the door. 'Hey, well done, Luke, that was all right. I'll give you some more practice in the garden this weekend and you'll soon be putting the wind up old Dracula ...'

Jon hesitated as his cousin was making frantic signs to him to shut up. 'Oh, hi, Sanjay,' he faltered. 'Er, didn't see you standing there ...'

'I gathered that,' the goalkeeper replied, shooting Luke a very black look before brushing roughly past Jon into the building.

'Right, men. All ready?' Luke demanded, holding the door handle.

'Ready, Skipper!' the Swifts responded automatically as part of their pre-match ritual before leaving the changing room.

'OK, follow me, let's go!' Luke yanked on the door and almost went through it face-first when it failed to budge.

'Er, I think you'll find it opens the other way, Skipper,' piped up Titch, Swifts' under-sized, midfield scrapper.

His partner on the left of midfield, Sean, a stylish passer of a ball, was still finishing combing his hair in the small mirror on the wall. 'Do you think we might have one of these put up in our cabin at home, Skipper?' he asked when the hilarity had subsided at Luke's bungled exit.

'No chance!' laughed Tubs. 'You'd spend so much time in front of the mirror, we'd never get you out on the pitch.'

Luke shoved the door this time, without too much more success. The door inched open, its base catching and scraping on the narrow wooden verandah that ran along the front of the old hut. 'Come and give me a hand, somebody. The useless thing is sticking.'

Sean saw his chance for revenge. 'Let Tubs put his weight behind it. He'll never squeeze through a gap like that.'

'I can get my belly through anything your head will fit,' Tubs snorted, and then nearly broke the rickety door off its hinges as he shoulder-charged his way past Luke.

'C'mon, men,' the skipper rallied them. 'This lot can't be much cop, playing at a dump like this.'

'Perhaps this is that cowshed you were telling us about!' Mark grinned.

The Swifts trooped out wearing their smart

all-gold strip that Luke had recently won for them in a soccer magazine competition. Its title logo was splashed in large green capital letters on their shirt-fronts: *GREAT GAME!*

Only Sanjay still wore his own kit, preferring his snazzy, multi-coloured top to the sponsored one. 'I'll show 'em all today!' he vowed under his breath as he jumped up to touch the crossbar, a lucky habit of his. 'They ain't seen nothing yet!'

'Look at them in black and white stripes,' cried Big Ben, pointing to the other end of the pitch where the home team were already warming up. 'It's like playing against the Comp.'

'Guess that's why they call themselves the Zebras,' said Mark.

'The grass is certainly long enough to graze on,' added Gary. 'We could lose Titch in this!'

Luke lost something else first, the toss, and the Swifts had to defend a rough, rutted penalty area. 'Watch the bounce, Sanjay,' he called. 'The ball could do strange things on a surface like this.'

'I know what I have to do,' the keeper replied pointedly. 'You just see to your job and I'll do mine, OK?'

'Part of my job as skipper is to make sure everybody knows theirs,' Luke reminded him. 'Only trying to help.'

Sanjay was tested out immediately. A hopeful, long-range drive was pumped goalwards in the opening minute and the ball hit one of the bumps, eluding Sanjay's hands. He'd succeeded in getting his body in line with the shot, however, and the ball cannoned off him for a corner.

'Well saved,' Luke praised him, coming back to stand on the line as an extra defender. 'Nasty one, that.'

'No sweat. Just leave things to me.'

His defenders did exactly that when the

corner came over high and long into the goal-mouth. 'Keeper's ball!' yelled Sanjay to make sure any Swifts' players kept out of his way as he leapt up to claim it. But a tall Zebras' attacker went for it, too, and timed his jump fractionally better, meeting the ball first and deflecting it downwards.

Luke blocked its path to goal. The skipper intended to chest the ball away to one side, but it bounced up awkwardly and struck his hand.

'Penalty!' screamed the Zebras.

The referee had to agree. Luke's hand had prevented the ball going over the line. The official pointed to the spot and blew his whistle.

'Accidental, ref!' Luke cried, but it was no use.

'Don't argue with me, son, or I'll take your name,' the man said.

'Great start, Skipper, thanks a bunch!' said Tubs.

'Don't worry, Tubs,' said Sanjay. 'He's just wanting to see how I save penalties. You watch, I'll give him something to practise all right in his back garden.'

To everyone's amazement, the goalkeeper positioned himself not in the centre of his goal, but near the left-hand post instead.

'Ready, keeper?' the referee asked. 'We're waiting.'

'Sure, ready when you are, ref. Just blow that whistle.'

'What's he playing at, standing there?' hissed Big Ben. 'Is this another of your stupid ideas?'

Luke shook his head. 'Nothing to do with me. Sanjay does things his own way when he's in this kind of mood.'

The penalty-taker seemed nonplussed as well. He glanced at the referee for help. 'Can he do that, ref? Is that fair?'

'It's up to him. He can stand where he likes so long as he's on his line and doesn't move before you kick the ball.'

None of the players had ever seen anything like it. The goalkeeper was crouched next to the post, leaving virtually the whole of the goal for the kicker to aim at. Advice rang out from behind his back.

'Just blast it wide of him. He'll never reach it.'

'You could roll it in and he wouldn't get across in time.'

'Watch it, he's getting ready to dive.'

'He's bluffing. Just sidefoot it in and make him look a nutcase.'

'You can't miss!'

As the whistle sounded, the boy ran in, hesitantly, still trying to make up his mind what to do. He couldn't resist looking at the goalie who had now straightened up and was actually grinning at him. Despite his nerves, the shooter struck the ball cleanly and sent it exactly where he aimed – right into the goalie's stomach! Sanjay never had to move an inch.

The boy cried out in dismay. 'He had to make a dive across. He just had to.'

But Sanjay didn't. He stood there now, ball snug in his gloves, hugely pleased with himself that his bold plan had worked so perfectly. Then he was mobbed by his relieved teammates.

'Incredible!' Dazza whooped. 'You totally psyched him out.'

'Fantastic, Dracula!' laughed Gary. 'You're well crazy!'

As they began to break away to continue the game, the penalty-taker was left still squatting down, unable to believe what had just happened to him. Luke shook Sanjay's outstretched hand. 'Brill, Sanjay. Wish I'd thought of that. Absolutely wicked!'

'Thanks, Skipper. You'll have to try it some time perhaps . . .'

'Not while you're here,' he winked. 'When are you going to get it into that thick head of yours that I'm not wanting to take your place. You're the main man, Sanjay!'

The goalkeeper grinned and half-turned, jabbing at the large white figure on the back of his top. 'That's right, I'm the number one!'

5 Great Game!

Sanjay had struck a huge psychological blow for the Swifts.

The penalty miss so early in the game, in so bizarre a fashion, caused some of the Zebras' players to feel it wasn't going to be their day. They knew the Swifts were bottom of the table, but already began to doubt whether they could ever beat such an amazing goalkeeper.

This belief was strengthened when Sanjay made no effort to go for another shot that seemed to be sailing wide, but swerved and struck the inside of the post instead. It bounced across the goal-line and ricocheted off the opposite post into the goalkeeper's welcoming embrace.

He nonchalantly threw the ball out to Sean to start an attack of their own, and space opened up in front of the midfielder as he flitted forwards deep into Zebras' territory. Sean timed his pass beautifully, slipping it inside the full-back for Brain to collect in his stride. The left winger was faced with a choice. He had time to lob the ball over to where Gregg and Luke, arms raised, were both loudly demanding it or to try a shot himself. He couldn't decide so he simply hit and hoped.

The Zebras' goalie was rooted in no-man's-land, off his line and trying to cover both centre or shot. He did neither. The ball spiralled up out of his reach, too far ahead of the attackers as well, and clipped the underside of the bar on its way into the net.

'Unstoppable!' cried Luke, the first to congratulate the scorer.

'Yeah, pity you didn't mean it to go there,' laughed Gregg.

'They all count,' said Brain.

'Dead right,' said Luke. 'Doesn't matter how they go in, as long as they do. We're one–nil up!'

The fact that they were still ahead at half-time was due to a further piece of goalkeeping extravaganza. A shot from outside the penalty area, which had Sanjay moving to his right, took a vicious deflection off Mark's knee. The ball changed direction abruptly and looped towards the top left-hand corner of the goal, only to be clawed out of the air by Sanjay's acrobatic about-turn. He twisted back like a piece of elastic and launched himself high enough to make the vital

contact. It was a reflex save that had all the spectators applauding, home team supporters and visitors alike.

'Save of the season!' enthused Dazza as they gathered together at the interval, but Sanjay accepted the praise uncharacteristically modestly.

'Just doing my job,' he said simply.

'What do we do now, Mr Crawford?' said Brain.

'Better ask the lad,' Luke's dad smiled. 'I'm only here so you've got somebody to stand around during the break like other teams!'

They waited for the skipper to rattle on as usual about battling away, not giving up and trying their hardest. For once, however, Luke was strangely hesitant. 'Er, I'm not quite sure what to say. I mean, we've never actually been in front before, like, at half-time!'

The shock of it finally came home to the players. 'It must be a dream!' said Big Ben. 'Wake me up somebody and tell me the score is really five–nil to them. I can cope with that.'

'Yeah, if we're not careful,' Sean warned, 'we might be in danger of destroying our reputation of being the worst team in the world.'

Luke stirred himself at last. 'Nonsense, this is the moment we've been waiting for all season, men, ever since we formed the Swifts. But don't take anything for granted. We've got to keep going right to the end . . .'

Luke was off into his usual spiel and everyone smiled, happy that things seemed normal once more. Things felt even more normal when, within five minutes of the re-start, they were in the familiar role of losing.

Sanjay could do nothing about the equalizer, a low shot drilled wide of him through a ruck of bodies after a corner. But he let himself down with the second goal, diving to hold the shot but then letting the ball dribble from his grasp and over the line.

He was so angry at his lapse that he snatched the ball out of the net and lashed it across the pitch to disappear into one of the nearby gardens. The goalkeeper had time to cool off, however, when the referee insisted that he go and climb over the fence and fetch the ball himself.

Luke, meanwhile, was summarising the reversal of fortunes into his make-believe microphone: *'The Swifts, tragically, now trail two–one*

after Sanjay's blunder, a cruel blow following such a promising first-half. It will be up to Luke Crawford, their experienced skipper, to lead by example and inspire his men to fight back and take control of this game again . . .'

Sadly, Luke's example was not quite of the kind intended. Set free on a run towards goal by Tubs' long clearance, Luke could not get the lively ball under control on the uneven surface. Long tufts of grass restricted his first attempt to shoot and when he managed to have another go, the ball popped up off a rut inside the area. He got his boot underneath the shot and the ball soared into the sky, high, wide and ugly. Luke even spared his commentary the pain of having to describe that effort.

It came as a surprise, therefore, when the Swifts did manage to draw level. Especially because the scorer was Titch – with a header!

As Brain's cross from the left touchline was flicked on by Gregg to the far post, the keeper was poised to gather it safely up. Suddenly, as if from nowhere, a little darting figure threw himself full-length – in Titch's case, not a great distance – in front of the keeper's chest to head the ball virtually out of his hands and into the net.

It was Titch's first-ever goal, in any form of football. He lay on the ground, stunned, until Tubs lifted him up and carried him bodily back to the half-way line like a prize exhibit.

Luke saw the referee glance at his watch. *'Time's nearly up, and it looks as if the Swifts will have to settle for the draw in the end. At least that breaks their duck and gives them their first point . . .'*

His tired commentary was unduly pessimistic. When they won a corner on the right, Luke signalled Brain over to try and swing the ball into the goalmouth. 'One last chance, men,' the skipper urged, 'but we don't want to get caught on the break. Hold back, defence, make sure we've got plenty of cover, just in case. Concentrate.'

He never even considered Sanjay. Luke's jaw dropped down to his knees when he realized a gangling, galloping goalkeeper was charging upfield to join in the fun. The Zebras could not believe their eyes either. The bright, multi-coloured top stood out clearly from the other shirts and their defensive organization fell apart. Nobody knew who was to mark him.

'Get back, Sanjay, get back!' Luke screamed, glancing fearfully at the Swifts' empty goal.

'What are you doing here? Have you gone mad?'

It was too late. Brain whipped the corner over, curling the ball in towards the near post. Sanjay timed his arrival perfectly and barely had to jump. He brushed past an uncertain challenger and sent a bullet header screaming over the fullback who was guarding the line.

When their victory had had time to sink in later, Luke composed his regular report for the village's free newspaper, the *Swillsby Chronicle*. Such indulgence was only permitted because it was edited by Uncle Ray.

SWIFTS TASTE SWEET VICTORY

by our soccer correspondent

Zebras 2 – 3 Swifts

Goalkeeper Sanjay Mistry was one of the many heroes as Swillsby Swifts snatched a memorable away victory to ease the threat of relegation. He turned from goal-stopper to goal-grabber in the dying seconds of the game, when skipper and coach Luke Crawford masterminded one last-ditch assault. 'It was death or glory,' Luke commented afterwards about the rare sight of a goalie joining the attack at a corner. But the daring gamble paid off. The Zebras panicked as if a lion had leapt into the middle of their herd!

Sanjay's dramatic winning header followed goals by Brian 'Brain' Draper and Tim 'Titch' Freeman after the Swifts seemed in danger of squandering a 1–0 interval lead. This was a match that truly lived up to the logo on the front of their shirts – *Great Game!* – and the

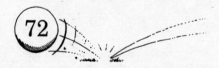

team's player-manager was full of confidence for the future. 'Now we've got our first league win under our belts,' he smiled, 'the only way is up!'

Luke was not the only one to find himself in print the following week. Sanjay's name appeared underneath a limerick in the poetry section of the monthly school magazine.

To be a Goalkeeper

There was a young goalie for Swills
Who displayed all the goalkeeping skills.
He might have been crazy
But not sloppy or lazy.
Crowds sure got excitement and thrills!

Sanjay Mistry (13) – 8C

The other boys had a problem. They had a double target for their wit and didn't know which writer to ridicule more, Luke for his pompous match report in the *Chronicle*, or Sanjay for his ludicrous limerick. Luke was grateful to Sanjay for switching their attack away from him temporarily.

73

'Swills?' Tubs snorted. 'Makes us sound like those pigs of Luke's!'

'Well, I couldn't think of anything to rhyme with Swillsby,' smirked Sanjay. 'Nor Swifts or the Comprehensive.'

Tubs considered the matter. 'Hmm, I can see what you mean.'

Out of Sanjay's earshot, Matthew and Adam were more scathing. 'Huh! He'll never be lazy playing for the Sloths,' grunted the captain. 'He's too busy picking the ball out of the back of the net all the time.'

'He's well named, though, isn't he? Mistry.'
Adam chuckled in the build-up to his own joke.
'It's a *mystery* how he keeps his place for the
Comp, the number of sloppy mistakes he makes
to cost us goals!'

Matthew grinned. 'Yeah, I just wish we had
somebody else to put in.'

Jon joined them at that point. 'Oh, you've
already heard the news then, I gather.'

'What news?' Matthew demanded.

'About Sanjay not being able to play for the
school on Saturday . . .'

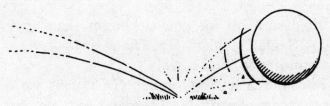

6 Super-Sub?

'Do you have to be away this weekend?' pleaded Gary. 'I mean, you'll miss the Swifts' game as well as the school's.'

Sanjay nodded. 'It's a big family do in London. Been hoping to get out of it and stay here, but I can't. You'll all just have to try and manage without me somehow.'

The goalkeeper was secretly pleased that his enforced absence seemed to be causing such problems. Frosty's squad practice was being devoted to finding an emergency replacement, and Sanjay smiled as he heard other boys making excuses why they could not play in goal.

'Who do you suggest could do the job?' Gary asked him.

'Matthew's not too bad, I suppose.'

'Yeah, but he doesn't want to. He says the captain should be out on the pitch. What about Tubs?'

'He'd sure fill the goal up better than anybody!' Sanjay laughed. 'Trouble is, it takes him ten minutes to bend down!'

Frosty was having similar discussions with his two best players, Matthew and Jon. 'Do you fancy having a go?' he asked the captain.

'Sorry, sir, but I went in goal once last season, remember, when Sanjay was away. And I've still got the scar on my chin to prove it!'

'What about Luke, sir?' Jon suggested. 'He's been practising real hard and he'd give his right arm for the chance to play.'

'That's all we need, a one-armed goalie!' Matthew sniggered.

Frosty shuddered at the thought. He had too many painful memories of Luke's chaotic appearances on the field to trust him in goal, likening this Crawford more to Jonah, rather than Johan, as a bringer of bad luck.

Almost everybody had to take a turn in goal

during the practice game, with Luke sneaking as many goes as he could, desperate to impress. But it was the reluctant Adam whom the teacher plumped for in the end, even though his presence at the heart of the defence would be sorely missed.

The disappointed Luke had to be content with a role as substitute. 'Can't promise you'll come on, but you never know,' Frosty said to him, deliberately handing him the number thirteen shirt. 'Bring that and a goalie top, if you've got one, and we'll see how things go.'

Luke had a top ready and waiting. He'd already tried out the Swifts' one that Sanjay didn't use, intending to wear it for his goalkeeping debut. If Frosty ignored him, as expected, at least nobody could stop him picking himself in goal on Sunday. He was surprised how much he was looking forward to that, considering his passion for playing as an attacker.

He felt good in the Swifts' new green top – and reckoned he looked the part in it too. He'd been admiring himself in his bedroom mirror, hurling himself on to the bed to save imaginary shots until Mum called upstairs to tell him to stop trying to break the springs.

Saturday dawned wet and windy, and the team arrived at Markham High School to find themselves pointed towards a small pitch in the far corner of the playing fields. 'It's a bit of a soggy trek, I'm afraid,' their teacher said. 'Hope your supporters have got their wellies and brollies!'

The players needed them as well. They were wet through even before the game started and Frosty wasn't best pleased either. He was having to act as referee, when he would much rather have been huddled in his overcoat underneath his great golfing umbrella – or better still, tucked up in bed.

'Why do I let myself in for this torture?' he mused as he blew the whistle for the match to kick off. The next thing he knew he was on his bottom. He'd slipped in the centre-circle mud-bath as he turned and was the only one who didn't find his discomfort hilariously funny.

The match started badly for the Swillsby team too. No, that's wrong. The match started disastrously. They went three goals down in the first ten minutes with Adam hardly touching the ball apart from fetching it from the hedge each time Markham scored. There were no nets, and each

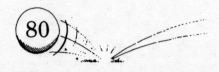

time he trudged off he became more bad-tempered.

'I've had enough,' he complained. 'Somebody else will have to go in.'

'Well, I'm not having Loony Luke,' the captain snarled. 'Stay in a bit longer. Things are bound to improve.'

They didn't. The home team continued to pile on the pressure and kept Swillsby pegged back into their own half with one attack after another. When the fourth goal went in, Matthew decided that drastic measures were called for. The captain swapped shirts with Adam.

Matthew was a natural soccer player who could perform well in any position, but he hated playing in goal. He soon hated it even more when a fifth was headed past him, and especially after he took a nasty crack on the leg preventing a certain sixth.

At half-time the players were drenched and

demoralised, milling around an equally depressed Frosty like a bunch of bedraggled beggars seeking shelter. 'Can't you abandon the game, sir?' Matthew moaned.

Frosty was sorely tempted, but something in his stubborn, professional pride insisted that the match must run its full course. At least it had stopped raining. 'No, let's see what kind of stuff you're made of,' he said. 'Show some character. Don't let them walk all over you.'

'But we're playing into the wind now as well,' the captain whined. 'We're going to get massacred!'

'Come back, Sanjay, all is forgiven,' Adam muttered.

'We've still got one keeper willing and eager,' said Jon, and no-one was in any doubt as to whom he meant.

Frosty scratched his head and took a deep breath. 'OK, Luke, get your coat off and . . .' he began, but the substitute was already stripped for action, a huge grin across his excited, flushed face. 'Er, right, good, so looks like you're in goal, then, second half.'

Matthew, restored to midfield, muttered a little mocking prayer. 'For what we are about to receive . . .'

Luke's clean kit did not stay that way for long. His very first dive saw him ending up face-first in a pool of dirty water. He missed the ball, but it missed the goal, too, skidding centimetres outside the upright. 'Had it covered,' he claimed. 'Knew it was going wide, so I left it.'

He left the next shot, too, but that was a total misjudgement. The ball flashed inside the post this time and it was Luke's turn to plod to the hedge to retrieve it.

The wind had gained in strength since the interval, and Jon and his fellow forwards spent

most of their time tracking back to try and help out their hard-pressed defence. They were all keen to prevent too many shots being aimed in Luke's direction.

One effort came out of the blue, however, and caught everyone by surprise – including Luke, of course. It came from his opposite number, enjoying a rare touch of the ball and intending to make the most of it.

The home goalkeeper knew this short pitch well. Standing on the edge of his penalty area, he gauged the force of the wind, tossed the ball up out of his hands and leathered it for all he was worth. The ball sailed into orbit and didn't return to earth until it bounced just outside the Swillsby area. No-one went for it, not particularly wanting to get their head underneath the dropping bomb.

Luke had been stationed on the penalty spot, shouting out his orders, and failed to appreciate the imminent danger. 'Mark up, men. Get goal-side of that winger, Gary. Watch this ball, Adam, it's a long one . . .'

'You watch it!' Adam shrieked. 'Watch the bounce!'

Luke ran forward at first, realized he couldn't

get near the ball and then began to back-pedal furiously as it reared up high again, heading goalwards. He lost his footing and crumpled into the mud, but still managed to follow the arc of the ball from his horizontal viewpoint as it spiralled down onto the top of the crossbar and flipped over out of play.

'Phew!' he breathed. 'That could have been very embarrassing!'

He let Adam take the ground kick. His own just weren't strong enough to send the ball out of the penalty area. Even Adam couldn't boot it very far and the defender hit the ball out of play as the safest option.

The winger took the throw quickly, though, hurling it into the path of his overlapping full-back. The boy sped down the line and clipped the ball beautifully into the middle. It deserved a goal, but the attackers never had a chance to get on the end of the cross. Luke beat them to it, leaping and punching the ball away. Not a very powerful punch, it was true, but enough to deflect it beyond them for Gary to complete the clearance.

Luke had decided the ball was too wet and slippery to try and catch. Even perfectly dry,

he suspected he would not have held on, so he elected to fist it instead, as he'd read about in the coaching manuals. Not textbook, but effective, and it won him the grudging praise of Adam.

'Better than I could have done,' the centre-back admitted.

That was all Luke desired. It did his personal confidence the power of good. For five minutes, he had a golden period. Things went his way and he rode his luck, making two more saves, fumbling another shot round the post and seeing a volley smack against the same post and fly away.

It couldn't last. Just when he began to think he might survive further horrors, the fates conspired against him. His quick drop-kick from his crowded goalmouth after a corner was intended to catch the home team out. But Luke was too hasty, took his eye off the ball and sliced his clearance. The ball struck the retreating Frosty on the back of the neck and rebounded cruelly into the goal.

As their opponents laughed their way to the centre-circle for the re-start, the Swillsby players looked at each other in bewilderment. 'That can't count, sir, surely!' Adam insisted.

'Course it does!' Frosty snapped, rubbing his neck. 'It's gone in, hasn't it?'

'Who gets the credit?' smirked Matthew, past caring about the result.

'Credit!' growled the teacher, sounding even more than usual like a bear with a sore head. 'Ask the *Chronicle*'s soccer correspondent. He's the expert round here on useless information about football!'

Luke sighed. 'Guess it goes down as an own goal,' he said after Frosty slouched off. 'I was the last one to kick the ball and refs can't score.'

'That's all right, then,' said Matthew, chuck-
ling.

'How do you mean?' asked Luke, expecting the
captain to be angry.

'I'd hate to have to confess to the other guys at
school that we were so bad, even Frosty got one
against us!'

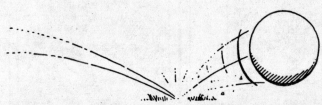

7 Insult and Injury

'So you missed me, then?' grinned Sanjay before Monday morning Assembly.

'Course we did. None of us can play in goal quite like you.'

Sanjay considered whether Luke was trying to be funny. 'I'll take that as a compliment,' he said. 'Adam told me the final result was nine–nil. Said you did all right in the end, though.'

'Could have been worse,' Luke conceded. 'They only scored two more after Frosty's back header. I think they must have got fed up or something or it might have been like yesterday's rout.'

'What happened to the Swifts?' Sanjay asked, eager for more tales of crushing defeats. 'Not heard anything yet. Nobody's mentioned it.'

'Not surprised.'

'Bad, was it?' he said, trying to hide his satisfaction.

Luke nodded, half turning away. 'Don't really want to talk about it.'

Sanjay yanked him back. 'C'mon, don't leave me in suspense. What was the score, man?'

Luke swallowed hard before answering. 'Twenty-five–nil.'

Sanjay repeated the score in amazement. 'Did you let all those in?'

'No,' Luke sighed but then couldn't keep up the act any longer and grinned. 'Nobody did. Our game was cancelled, you nutter. Too much rain. Ground waterlogged!'

Sanjay laughed at being taken in so easily. 'Just as well perhaps. Anyway, hope the weather's OK for next Sunday against Ashton.'

'You don't normally know who we're playing till I tell you,' Luke said, seeming surprised at Sanjay's sudden knowledge of their fixture list. 'What's so special about Ashton Athletic?'

'I played for them for two seasons.'

'Oh, right, I remember now. That's useful. You can fill us in about their weaknesses. Do you still know their players?'

'Yeah, good mates of mine.'

'So why did they get rid of you?' Luke asked cheekily. 'Wouldn't be anything to do with the fact that they got relegated last year, would it?'

'No, it wasn't,' Sanjay protested. 'I left, if your memory's failing, because you begged me to come and play for the Swifts.'

'Suppose you'll want to play in goal against them in that case?'

Luke's remark was phrased as a question, but Sanjay sensed something more behind it. A dark hint of a threat to his position.

'You bet I do. I'm gonna show them what they're missing.'

'Don't expect they've forgotten your style of goalkeeping already!'

'What d'yer mean by that?' he demanded. 'I *am* playing, aren't I?'

'Sure,' Luke replied. 'It's just that, well, I kind of enjoyed it in goal for the school. I was sorry our game was called off. I fancied a bit more practice between the sticks.'

'Come on, Luke, you can't be serious. I've *got*

94

to be in goal against Ashton. I know it's your
team, but if you don't pick me as keeper, that's
it, finished. I won't ever play for you again!'

Sanjay stormed off, close to tears in his rage,
barging past Tubs and Big Ben in the corridor
without even seeing them.

'What's got into old Dracula?' Tubs asked.

Luke affected a shrug. 'He's threatened to
walk out on the Swifts!'

Big Ben was mad, too, when Luke explained
what had happened. 'He's been going on about

this match for weeks. You must have known how much he was looking forward to it.'

'Course I did, I hadn't forgotten about him playing for Ashton,' Luke grinned. 'I was just pulling his leg. Firing him up a bit. Making sure he's really motivated to be on top form.'

'A dangerous game, that, if you ask me,' muttered Tubs. 'What if he refuses to play now just out of spite?'

'He won't,' Luke said confidently, 'because I'm going to make him an offer he can't refuse.'

'What's that?' snapped Big Ben.

'I'm going to let him be captain for the day against his old club. It's a sort of tradition in football. He won't be able to resist it.'

'I still don't see why you had to go getting him all riled up.'

Luke tapped his nose knowingly. 'As one of the pigs in *Animal Farm* said, it's tactics. It's what good management is all about, trying to get the best out of your players.'

'Well, I just hope you know what you're doing,' said Tubs.

Luke wandered off, feeling quite pleased with himself. 'Oh, I know, all right,' he mused. 'Sanjay is bound to play out of his skin as skipper – but

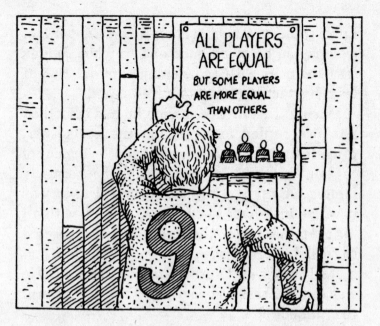

he's had a little reminder who the real boss is!'

Luke arrived early at the cabin before the Swifts' mid-week practice, making sure that no-one saw him pin up an extra poster. As the players were changing, they kept glancing quizzically at the wall.

Dazza had finished Orwell's story in English and nudged Sanjay with his elbow. 'Seen that?'

Underneath the statement '*All Players Are Equal*' was now the pointed amendment: '*But Some Players Are More Equal Than Others*'.

Luke could not help feeling a certain pang of jealousy as he stood back and watched Sanjay toss the coin with the Ashton captain. But at least his tactic seemed to have worked.

During the practice session he had smoothed Sanjay's ruffled feathers and the goalkeeper, pride restored, was quick to accept the honour of captaincy. Luke had never seen the normally laid-back Sanjay so keyed up to do well as he was now. He may have been fooling around with all his old mates before the match as they inspected the dried-out Swillsby pitch, but Sanjay also had a steely glint of determination in his eyes. He was out to prove to everybody that he was still the number one.

'Change round, team,' Sanjay called out. 'I've won the toss. I want the wind behind us second half.'

Ashton seemed equally positive. Nothing was going to please them more than defeating the Swifts and putting plenty of goals past their former keeper into the bargain. 'C'mon, the Reds!' cried their captain, Daniel. 'We've only got Sanjay to beat. And you know how easy that is.'

They set out the way they meant to carry on, cutting ruthlessly through the Swifts' porous

98

defence like an electric saw through a mound of jelly. But inside the wobbly dessert, they found a hard nut to crack – Sanjay.

The goalkeeper was inspired. Whatever Ashton Athletic threw at him, he caught it, punched it, blocked it, dived on it and smothered it – and threw it back at them to try again. Once he even headed a shot off the line.

'Look, Daniel, no hands!' he laughed. 'That's how *easy* it is!'

Luke was also in full flow, at least with his babbling commentary. The words gushed out of him like water from a burst pipe: '*A massive kick from Sanjay, having the game of his life, finds Brain free on the left wing. He holds the ball, relieving the pressure for a time, and then switches play across the field to Dazza on the right. The long pass has caught Ashton flat-footed, but Dazza still needs help. It's offered by the player-manager, Luke Crawford, always on hand to provide support . . . Uughh!*'

Luke was up-ended unceremoniously from behind. Not because he was in a dangerous position, but more because his marker could not bear to listen any longer to his biased commentary. The foul had the desired effect to some

degree, silencing Luke briefly, but the free-kick was not so merciful. Titch took it smartly while Luke was still limping about, Gregg shot and the rebound was rifled home by Dazza from an acute angle.

While the visitors were recovering from that unexpected setback, the Swifts scored again, Gregg himself this time polishing off a move started by Dazza. The 2–0 lead was a travesty of justice and it only served to make Ashton re-double their efforts to put the record straight. By half-time, the scoreline told a different, fairer story.

Despite all his heroics, Sanjay could do little to prevent the first two goals that finally found his net, one high, one low, but both into unreach-able corners. And when the third came as a result of a frantic goalmouth scramble, in which the keeper-captain twice excelled himself with brave stops, the Swifts' woes were complete. Sanjay was injured.

Attempting to claw the ball back from going over the line, the goalkeeper had his fingers crushed accidentally under a player's boot. Friend or foe, it wasn't clear, but the damage was just the same.

'There's no way you can carry on in goal,' Luke's uncle said at half-time, which fortunately came soon after the incident. 'My advice is that you go straight home and get that right hand seen to properly.'

'What, and miss the rest of the match?' gasped Sanjay, clearly in pain but not willing to admit how much. 'Forget it! I'm staying.'

'But you can't keep goal like that.'

'I'll play out on the pitch then. I'm not coming off.'

'What do you think, Luke?' asked Uncle Ray.

Luke didn't have a chance to reply. 'He's not skipper today, I am,' Sanjay said defiantly. 'So I decide what we do, right?'

Luke was tempted to quash that by saying he was still player-manager, but wisely bit his lip. 'So who goes in goal?' he asked simply.

'You do!' stated Sanjay. 'Anybody got any objections to Luke playing in goal?'

One or two almost spoke up, but recognized the mood was in Luke's favour and kept quiet. Big Ben voiced the majority feeling of the team. 'Luke's been practising at least. He knows what to do.'

Whether he could actually do it or not was

another matter, but any doubts were not expressed. Luke felt chuffed that he hadn't even had to volunteer or insist he went in goal. The others wanted him to, and that was the important difference.

Sanjay's goalie top came down to Luke's knees and he hastily stuffed it into his shorts before donning the gloves. They were too big as well, but he'd left his own at home.

'Right, men,' Luke said while Sanjay's head disappeared inside the number nine shirt. 'We may have gone and thrown away a two-goal lead, but we don't intend to lose this game. C'mon, let's go out there now and win it for Sanjay!'

8 Seven-a-Side

It was the most mad-cap, see-saw second half. The two sides slugged it out tirelessly, trading goals like swapping football stickers.

The Swifts opened the scoring at both ends. Gregg gave his team the ideal start by putting them back on level terms in their very first attack, blasting home a neat pass from Sean. But this was quickly cancelled out by Luke's second too – his second own goal in consecutive games. And this time he needed no help from the referee. It was all his own work.

Not trusting his kicking after the Frosty business, Luke decided to throw the ball out whenever he could. That was safer – or should have been. In Sanjay's large goalie gloves, however, his grip on the ball was not very secure. As he leant back to hurl it out to the wing, he lost control of the ball and it popped out of his right glove and rolled agonisingly over the goal-line before Luke could react.

'And he talks about throwing things away!' said Sean, shaking his head.

Luke threw the gloves away, too. He tossed them into the back of the net in disgust, preferring to rely on his bare hands. It was to no avail. Soon Ashton went 5–3 up as Daniel slid a low cross past a motionless Luke, still brooding over his gaffe.

The two captains briefly stood side-by-side before the re-start. 'Who's that dummy you've put in goal?' smirked Daniel. 'Has he been bribed to make sure you lose?'

Sanjay sighed. 'No need, he always does that anyway! He's the crazy guy I've told you about before, Luke Crawford. He runs this team.'

'Him!' scoffed Daniel. 'No wonder you're bottom of the league! With him in goal and you out on the pitch, we're going to run riot!'

'Don't count your chickens, you've not won yet,'

Sanjay retorted, just for the sake of it. He didn't even believe it himself. His dreams of a great victory over his former teammates had already been dashed.

At that point, the game might have gone away from the Swifts completely if Ashton had been allowed to score again – and this looked probable when an attacker burst clear through the middle of the Swifts' defence.

Their inexperienced keeper ventured out unsteadily to meet the oncoming opponent, trying to recall the advice in chapter three of *The Art and Craft of Goalkeeping*. Luke didn't want to commit himself too soon, staying on his feet until the last second and narrowing the shooting angle with every metre. The striker was forced to make the first move and the moment he did, intending to dribble round the keeper, Luke pounced and dived at his feet. Amazingly, he won the ball, gripping it tightly to his chest, but was badly winded too when the other boy fell heavily on top of him.

The referee halted the game while Luke recovered his breath, but he refused to let go of the ball. He'd got it and he meant to keep it, relishing the praise from his teammates.

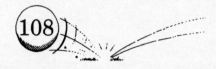

'Blinding save, Skip!' cried Dazza.

Even Sanjay was impressed. 'Good job you brought your protractor to work out all those angles,' he joked.

Then it was Sanjay's turn to bask in the glory limelight. The Draper–Mistry double act worked its magic once more, only this time Brain floated his corner right across the six-yard box for Sanjay's long legs to propel him high above his challengers. He met the ball square on his fore-head to power it into the same net he had fought so hard earlier to keep it out of.

Sanjay was overjoyed to score against his old pals, a reward that made him forget all about the tingling ache in his mangled fingers. He played a key part in the next goal, too, brought down outside the area in the defender's anxiety that Sanjay shouldn't be allowed to grab another. Brain did the rest, drilling the direct free-kick with deadly accuracy through the ramshackle wall of bodies and past the unsighted goal-keeper.

'What's the score, ref?' asked Sanjay. 'I've lost count.'

'Five–all, son – I think,' he replied uncertainly.

A little later, the official had to revise his calculations. The Swifts nosed ahead again, with Gregg notching their third successive goal and completing his personal hat-trick at the same time. He was set up unselfishly by his elder twin, who presented him with a simple tap-in goal when Gary himself might well have been tempted to add his own name to the ever-expanding scoresheet.

'Great stuff, I'm proud of you, junior!' yelled Gary into his ear as they celebrated together. He liked to remind Gregg every now and again that

111

he was ten minutes older and knew how using the term junior irritated his younger brother. It helped to keep Gregg in his place and stopped him from getting too big for his boots!

The Swifts had to be aware of the danger of falling into the same trap themselves. With so narrow a lead, this was no time for a display of over-confidence and Luke should have known better. After making a save, he went and spoiled his good work with a silly piece of bravado. He allowed his enthusiasm and excitement to run away with him, dropping the ball at his feet and dribbling it well beyond his area as if he were still playing out on the pitch. He hoped to be able to kick it further upfield and produce another goal, which it did, but not for the Swifts.

Luke had already seen Sanjay caught out, attempting something similar in the school game, but it didn't stop him repeating the error. Daniel put him under pressure, whipped the ball off his toes and lobbed it towards the vacant goal. Luke was the only player near enough to try and prevent a further humiliation and he hared after the bouncing ball at top speed.

His relief was enormous as the ball struck the post, but it rebounded towards him and Luke

was going too fast to get out of the way. He tried to jump over it but the ball hit his knee and bobbled back into the goal. Luke keeled over and finished up nursing the ball, upside-down, helplessly tangled in the netting by his studs.

'I don't believe it,' he groaned softly. 'Another stupid own goal!'

With only about five minutes remaining, both teams might have been happy to settle for a high-scoring draw, but the match had more stings left in its scorpion's tail.

Tubs was the next in line for match-winning, hero status with his first goal of the season, thumping a long-distance shot high into the roof

of the net. Sadly, the Swifts' delirious cele-
brations that followed were premature. Sanjay
was still to have a hand in the final outcome.

In their desperation not to lose, Ashton
pushed everybody forward in search of yet
another equalizer. In consequence, Swifts pulled
everybody back to try and hold them at bay and
protect their slender advantage. During a fren-
zied attack, perhaps obeying his natural
instincts, Sanjay found himself in his accus-
tomed position on the goal-line. The ball evaded
Luke's grasp and was destined for the net until
Sanjay dived across to his right and knocked it
away.

'Great save!' Mark said, helping Sanjay to his
feet. 'Just a pity you're not actually in goal!'

The referee considered sending Sanjay off for
the handling offence, but felt the boy had suf-
fered enough. He had hurt his bad fingers again
and went to sit down off the pitch behind the goal
in misery. Sanjay could do no more. The result
was now out of his control. The penalty was to be
the last kick of the match.

'It's all up to you, Luke!' he called out.

This was a total new experience for Luke. He
didn't much fancy his chances of saving Daniel's

penalty by normal methods. He decided on the spur of the moment to adopt Sanjay's previously successful tactics instead.

It had helped to bring the Swifts victory before and Luke reasoned that the same high-risk strategy might do so again. He stood poised by the side of the post and then began swaying, wanting Daniel to think he was going to hurtle across the goal.

'No, don't try that!' Sanjay cried in alarm. 'It won't work again.'

'Huh! Bet he doesn't want me to show I can do it too,' Luke grunted. 'With a bit of luck, Daniel will fall for it just like that other kid.'

Luke wasn't to know it , but he was going to need a lot of luck . . .

At the referee's signal, the Ashton captain ran in, ignoring the keeper's antics. He concentrated all his attention on placing the ball into the wide open space and struck it with the inside of his right boot. Bang on target. The kick was tucked into the far corner of the net and Luke never even moved. His mouth dropped open. Daniel hadn't followed the script. He was supposed to hit the penalty straight at him!

'Sorry, Skipper,' came the lame apology from

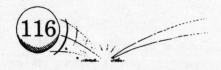

116

behind the goal. 'Me and my big mouth! I'd already bragged to him about that penalty stunt I pulled off against the Zebras.'

'You'd done what?' Luke gasped. 'Now you tell me!'

'I was trying to before, but . . .' Sanjay shrugged and started to titter. He couldn't help himself, and soon his infectious giggling spread to the other players, too, as they all caught on to the joke. Even Luke saw the funny side of what had just happened and joined in the laughter.

As the teams shook hands, the referee went over to the touchline. 'Do you make that seven

goals each?' he asked hopefully.

'Aye, a fair result,' agreed Ashton's manager. 'Nobody deserved to lose a roller-coaster of a match like that!'

'Nobody deserved to win it either,' Luke's dad chuckled. 'I reckon both teams were as bad as each other!'

Sanjay hung back in the changing cabin afterwards, taking his time and refusing any help in dressing with his sore fingers. He wanted to be the last to leave and waited until Luke had stepped outside to talk to his dad and uncle.

Sanjay checked through the doorway to make sure he was not going to be disturbed. Then he took out a thick black marker pen from his coat pocket and went up to the posters on the wall. He'd planned carefully what he was going to do, even before such manic performances from Luke and himself in the match. He wanted to get his own back for the skipper's recent rivalry and treatment of him.

'Good job my writing hand's OK,' Sanjay smiled. He crossed out four words on one of the posters and neatly printed his alternative choices above. He was just finishing his task as the door creaked open and he whirled round.

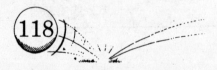

'I think we'd best leave it for our teammates to decide which is which, eh, Sanjay!' said Luke, admiring his pal's handiwork, and the two lads grinned at each other.

THE END

ABOUT THE AUTHOR

Rob Childs was born and grew up in Derby. His childhood ambition was to become an England cricketer or footballer – preferably both! – but, after graduating from Leicester University, he went into teaching and taught at primary and high schools in Leicester, where he now lives. Always interested in school sports, he coached school teams and clubs across a range of sports, and ran area representative teams in football, cricket and athletics.

Recognizing a need for sports fiction for young readers, he decided to have a go at writing such stories himself and now has more than thirty books to his name, including the popular *The Big Match* series, published by Young Corgi Books. *All Goalies are Crazy* is the second title in the *Soccer Mad* series.

Rob now combines his writing career with work helping dyslexic students (both adults and children) to overcome their literacy difficulties. Married to Joy, also a writer, Rob has a "lassie" dog called Laddie and is also a keen photographer.

SOCCER MAD
Rob Childs

'This is going to be the match of the century!'

Luke Crawford is crazy about football. A walking encyclopedia of football facts and trivia, he throws his enthusiasm into being captain of the Swillsby Swifts, a Sunday team made up mostly of boys like himself – boys who love playing football but get few chances to play in real matches.

Luke is convinced that good teamwork and plenty of practice can turn his side into winners on the pitch, but he faces a real challenge when the Swifts are drawn to play the Padley Panthers – the league stars – in the first round of the Sunday League Cup . . .

The first title in an action-packed new football series.

0 440 863449

SOCCER AT SANDFORD
Rob Childs

'We're going to have a fantastic season!'

Jeff Thompson is delighted to be picked as captain of Sandford Primary School's football team. With an enthusiastic new teacher and a team full of talent – not least that of loner Gary Clarke, with his flashes of goal-scoring brilliance – he is determined to lead Sandford to success. Their goal is the important League Championship – and their main rivals are Tanby, who they must first meet in a vital Cup-tie . . .

From kick-off to the final whistle, through success and disappointment, penalties and corners, to the final nail-biting matches of the season, follow the action and the excitement as the young footballers of Sandford Primary School learn how to develop their skills and mould together as a real team – a team who are determined to win by playing the best football possible.

0 440 86318 X

SANDFORD ON TOUR
Rob Childs

'We're on our way!' shouted Jeff. 'Let's go! Let's get at 'em!'

The footballers of Sandford Primary School are off on tour! Invited to take part in a major schools football tournament, an exciting six days is planned for the whole first team squad. Not only are they to take part in the tournament itself, but they are to play a couple of friendly matches on the way *and* have a go at a variety of other outdoor activities – including rock-climbing and caving.

It's a great chance for Sandford to show what they can do and Jeff Thompson, captain of the squad, can hardly wait to be off. But when they arrive at the tournament, they run up against the home team Waverley – a team who play as rough as they can get away with. And Waverley issue a challenge – a challenge that Sandford are determined to meet . . .

An action-packed and thrilling footballing tale – from the author of *Soccer at Sandford*.

0 440 863201

THE BIG MATCH
Rob Childs

'ACE SAVE, CHRIS!' shouted Andrew as his younger brother pushed yet another of his best shots round the post. 'You're unbeatable today.'

But will he be unbeatable when he is picked to stand in for the regular school team goalkeeper in a vital cup game against Shenby School, their main rivals? For Chris is several years younger than the rest of the team — and they aren't all as sure of his skill in goal as his older brother is . . .

A fast-moving and realistic footballing story for young readers.

0 552 524514